A Sesame Street Toddler Book

I Did It!

D1278599

Featuring Jim Henson's Sesame Street Muppets

By Anna Ross • Illustrated by Norman Gorbaty

Random House / Children's Television Workshop

Library of Congress Cataloging-in-Publication Data:
Ross, Anna. I did it! : featuring Jim Henson's Sesame Street Muppets / by Anna Ross ; illustrated by Norman Gorbaty.   p.   cm.–(A Sesame Street toddler book) SUMMARY: Little Bert, Little Cookie Monster, and the other Muppet toddlers are able to do many things, including stacking blocks, making cookies, sweeping trash, drawing, and sliding down the slide.   ISBN: 0-394-86019-5   [1. Growth–Fiction. 2. Puppets–Fiction] I. Gorbaty, Norman, ill. II. Title. III. Series. PZ7.R71962Iad   1990   [E]–dc20   89-34543

Manufactured in Italy   4 5 6 7 8 9 0

Little Bert was building
a tower with blocks.
Higher and higher he
stacked the blocks.
Taller and taller.
The tower teetered.

Crash! The block tower tumbled down.

"Oh, dear," said Little Bert.

Little Bert decided to try again. This time he put more blocks at the bottom. This time he stacked the blocks straighter at the top. This time he put a triangle block on the tippy top.

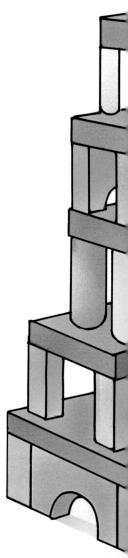

The tower stood tall.
It stood still.
"I did it!" said
Little Bert.

Little Cookie Monster was making cookies. He mixed and mixed until the dough was smooth.

He mashed and mashed until the cookies were flat.

He put on raisins
and cherries and peanuts
to make monster faces.
"Cowabunga!" cried
Cookie Monster.

He did it!
Then he gobbled
them up.

Little Bert was sweeping.
Sweep, sweep, swoosh!
The dirt and dead leaves
flew into the air.
Sweep, sweep, swoosh!
Down the steps swirled
the trash.

"All clean," said Little Bert.
"I did it!"
    "Hey, thanks," said Little Oscar.
"I love trash!"

Little Ernie was getting
dressed all by himself.
He pulled up his jeans.
He pulled down his shirt.

He pulled on his socks
and stuck his feet into
his sneakers.

"Hey, Bert," he called.
"I did it!"

Baby Alice was playing ball with Snuffy.
"Throw the ball to me!" she shouted.
"I can catch it."

"Oh, dear," said Snuffy. "What if I
bonk you on the snuffle?"

Snuffy threw the ball.

Bonk! The ball bounced on the sidewalk and into Alice's arms.

Thunk! She caught it with her snuffle.

"I did it, I did it!" cried Baby Alice.

Little Betty Lou was sharing her crayons
with Little Elmo.

"I wish I could draw," said Elmo.

"You can!" said Betty Lou.

Elmo made a yellow mark. Then he
scribbled some orange. Then he colored
some green.

"There!" said Little Elmo. "It's called 'Sunny Day.'
"I did it!"

Little Herry wanted
to slide down the slide.
But when he sat at the
top and looked down,
he couldn't do it.

"Hey! Hurry up, Herry!" shouted Little Oscar.

"Come on, Herry," said Little Bert. "Even I can go down the slide."

"You can do it, Herry!" Little Ernie said.

Herry took a deep breath. He shut his eyes and pushed. ZOOM! He felt a *woosh* in his fur.

When Little Herry opened his eyes, he was sitting at the bottom.

"Did you see that?" he said. "I did it!"